Contents

THE MYSTERIOUS TRAM

Jack and Emily discovered a tram stop that was so renowned in a town of wonder where mysteries abound. Those few curious people murmured about its existence.

A magical location where wishes might come true. They skipped and hopped toward the location where they believed the tram would arrive.

As they waited with waited with anticipation,a quirky conductor named Mr. Pockets appeared. With a twinkle in his eye, he invited the children to board the tram, promising an unforgettable journey. They eagerly hopped aboard, their hearts filled with excitement.

MEETING TALKING ANIMALS

Talking animals, with eyes shining bright wise old owl perched on a branch up high, With feathers so soft, it caught their eye."Hoo, young ones," it hooted, a riddle in its beak, Challenging their minds, making them think.

Many squirrels chattered away, full of energy and zest, As it hopped from tree to tree, a lively little guests. It shared secrets of the forest, hidden and unseen, A world of wonders, beyond what they had ever dreamed.

They suddenly passed by a very clever fox who has a lot of wisdom and stories to tell. Emily and Jack were overwhelmed by this new experience.

In this enchanted realm, where dreams come true,Animals spoke, sharing wisdom so true.Owls hooted riddles, foxes told tales.

DANCING WITH FAIRIES

The tram brought them to a grand meadow, Where fairies danced, a magical band. With delicate wings and dresses of hues, The fairies fluttered, their grace they'd infuse. Jack and Emily watched in awe and delight, As the fairies twirled, their spirits taking flight. The music played a sweet melody, Guiding their feet to join the fairies' fleet.

ADVENTURES UNVEILED

Next, the tram took them to a hidden cave, Where treasures glittered, ready to pave the path of excitement, discovery, and awe, As they searched for the gems that the legends saw.

With lanterns in hand, they ventured deep, Through tunnels and caverns, secrets to keep. Each step forward was a thrilling surprise,

As they uncovered treasures before their eyes. From shimmering crystals to ancient scrolls, The cave whispered stories that touched their souls They learned of bravery, of courage and might, And the power of believing in one's light.

As they emerged from the cave, the sun shining bright, Jack and Emily sibling's children felt a sense of delight. the cave had brought them adventures unveiled, With giants and treasures that would forever be hailed.

SPLASHING IN WATERFALL

In the land of enchantment, where dreams come alive, Jack and Emily's children dive Into a chapter of their wondrous escapade, Where waterfalls awaited, a magical cascade. With a skip and a hop, they followed the sound, Of rushing waters, where joy could be found.

A waterfall is so majestic, shimmering in the light. Its waters cascaded, like a silvery veil, Inviting them closer, without fail. They tiptoed on rocks, with excitement so grand, Feeling the mist, the water's gentle hand. With giggles and laughter, they splashed and played, In the waterfall's embrace, their worries allayed.

Onward they traveled, to a meadow so serene, Where unicorns grazed, their coats pristine. Majestic and noble, a sight to behold, They inspired wonder, these creatures.

Next, they journeyed to a waterfall grand, Where mermaids swam and frolicked, hand in hand. Their voices were like songs, as they danced in the mist, A mesmerizing sight that could not be missed.

FAREWELL TO THE MAGICAL TRAM

In a realm of enchantment, where dreams had come true, child Jack and Emily knew their journey was through. This had arrived, bringing bittersweet tears, As they neared the end, their hearts filled with fear. The magical tram, their faithful guide, Had taken them on a wondrous ride.

THE END

Printed in Great Britain
by Amazon